GLADIATOR BOY VS

THE CLONE WARRIORS

1. A HERO'S QUEST
2. ESCAPE FROM EVIL
3. STOWAWAY SLAVES
4. THE REBELS' ASSAULT
5. RESCUE MISSION
6. THE BLADE OF FIRE
7. THE LIVING DEAD
8. THE RAGING TORRENT
9. THE THREE NINJAS
10. THE INSANE FURY
11. THE WHITE SNAKE
12. THE GOLEM ARMY
13. THE SCREAMING VOID
14. THE CLONE WARRIORS
15. THE ULTIMATE EVIL

THE CLONE WARRIORS

DAVID GRIMSTONE

Hodder
Children's
Books

A division of Hachette Children's Books

First published in Great Britain in 2010
by Hodder Children's Books

A Catalogue record for this book is available from
the British Library

ISBN: 978 1 444 90087 3

Typeset by Tony Fleetwood

Printed and bound in Great Britain by CPI Bookmarque, Croydon

The paper and board used in this paperback by Hodder Children's Books are
natural recyclable products made from wood grown in
sustainable forests. The manufacturing processes conform to the
environmental regulations of the country of origin.

Hodder Children's Books
a division of Hachette Children's Books
338 Euston Road, London NW1 3BH
An Hachette UK company

www.hachette.co.uk

*For Charlie James, who should never be called
Charlotte to her face.*

I would like to dedicate the entire Gladiator Boy *series
to Terry Pratchett. There is no writer, living or dead,
for whom I have greater respect. Thank you
for everything.*

HOW MANY

GLADIATOR BOY

BOOKS DO YOU HAVE?

A HERO'S QUEST

ESCAPE FROM EVIL

STOWAWAY SLAVES

THE REBELS' ASSAULT

RESCUE MISSION

THE BLADE OF FIRE

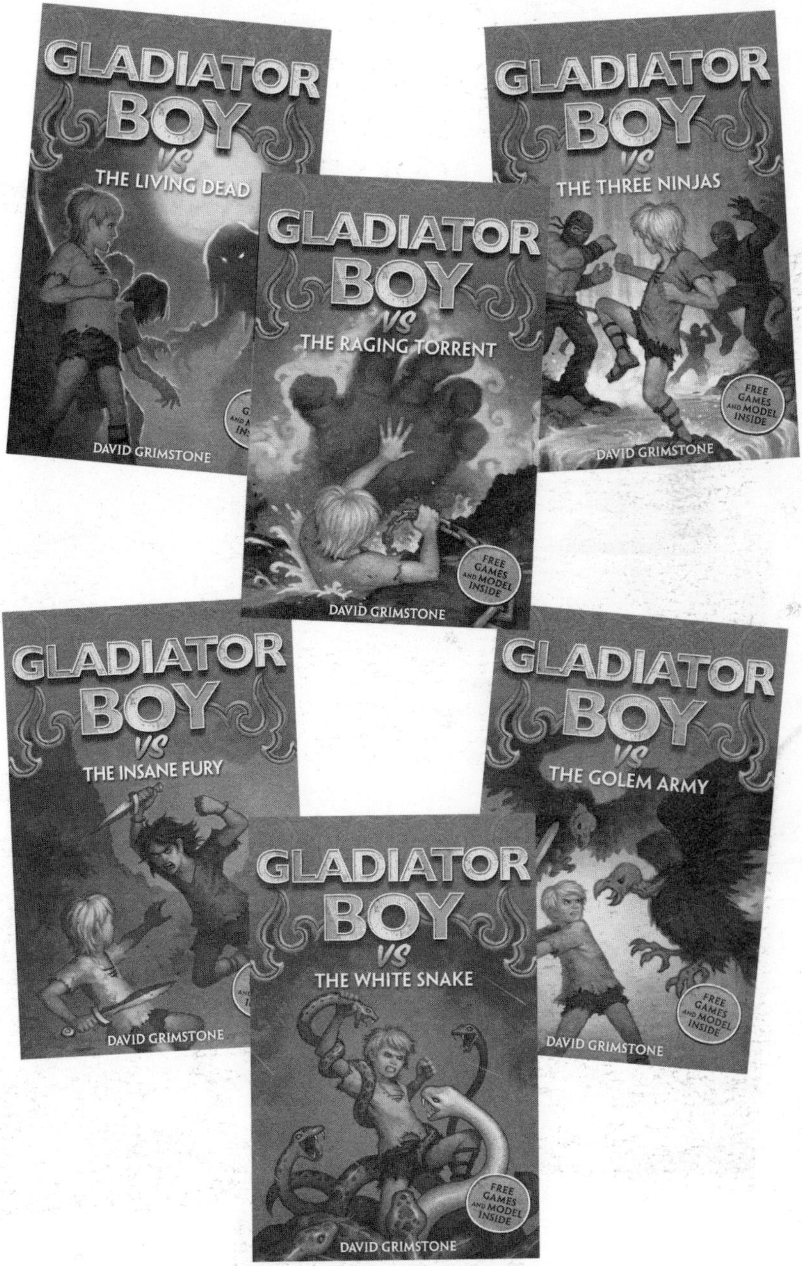
GLADIATOR BOY
VS
THE LIVING DEAD
DAVID GRIMSTONE
GLADIATOR BOY
VS
THE THREE NINJAS
FREE GAMES AND MODEL INSIDE
DAVID GRIMSTONE
GLADIATOR BOY
VS
THE RAGING TORRENT
FREE GAMES AND MODEL INSIDE
DAVID GRIMSTONE
GLADIATOR BOY
VS
THE INSANE FURY
DAVID GRIMSTONE
GLADIATOR BOY
VS
THE GOLEM ARMY
FREE GAMES AND MODEL INSIDE
DAVID GRIMSTONE
GLADIATOR BOY
VS
THE WHITE SNAKE
FREE GAMES AND MODEL INSIDE
DAVID GRIMSTONE

ITALY

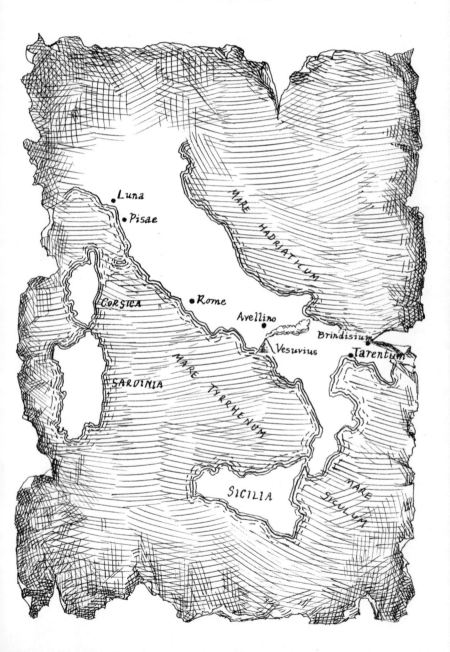

PREVIOUSLY IN GLADIATOR BOY

Decimus Rex has been captured by the dreaded Mirror Master, a man responsible for the kidnapping of hundreds of young children. In an effort to free their friend, the remaining slaves have entered the chasm of the Screaming Void, only to fall beneath the might of the primitive cavers and their evil commander, Captain Lich. Now, however, Lich has lost control of the horde of cavers . . . and a terrible battle is about to begin.

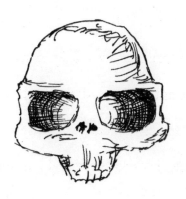

CHAPTER
I

THE
BATTLE
OF THE
VOID

Captain Andrus Lich stood in the middle of a glowing pool of light cast by more than a hundred flaming torches. In one hand he held the battered and bleeding form of Gladius and in the other he held a deformed monkey skull that had, until recently, contained a burning candle. Now, the flame had been blown out ... and with it had gone the power that Lich had used to enthral the cavers.

The beasts themselves, circling Captain Lich with a rebellious gleam flashing in their eyes, had abandoned their former captives and left the young slaves unconscious on the cavern floor.

Forming a greater circle around the cavers were the newly arrived soldiers of the Mirror Master's guard-army. Swords drawn, they

carefully moved in, eager to save their superior from attack but equally desperate not to start a fight they might not be able to win.

All eyes watched Captain Lich, and the big slave still struggling at his side.

'Stupid boy,' the captain snarled. 'Very, very stupid.'

Gladius licked his bloodied lips. 'I'd say it was smart – now you can't control them, can you?'

Captain Lich released his grip on Gladius, and belted the big slave hard in the face with a ragged fist.

Gladius collapsed, and the cavers moved nearer, their leader beginning to growl as the circle closed in.

Behind them, the outer group of soldiers also shifted towards the captain, slowly drawing swords as the beasts advanced for their master.

Seething in pain from Lich's strike, Gladius rolled over on the ground in front of the dread captain, and suddenly bellowed with all his might: 'CHARGE!'

The cavern exploded with frantic activity.

Certain the order had come from their master, the soldiers immediately flew at the cavers who – in their turn – took the cry as a challenge from Lich. They too lunged forward, and the chasm became a rioting, rampaging battleground.

Amidst the wreckage, Gladius forced himself on to all fours and attempted to scramble between the legs of the warring factions in order to reach his unconscious friends. However, he was trampled and kicked so often that he quickly found a fallen soldier and hunkered down beneath the unfortunate wretch, using his body as a shield of sorts.

Despite having only one working arm and a leg that was effectively no more than a wooden strut, Captain Lich was a devastating fighter. As the cavers charged in, he had drawn his own blade and set about them, spinning impossibly fast and carving his way through the horde without any sign of a controlled strategy. The rampaging soldier was a ball of wild energy, and his decrepit form had apparently done much to disguise the unyielding ferocity he fought with.

His crazed determination instilled the army of guards with a new confidence, and they no longer held back, crashing against the cavers in a storm of blades.

For their part, the primitive tribe fought only with their hands, but they possessed an almost limitless strength. In several places, cavers were actually snatching soldiers off their feet and *hurling* them into each other. Swords flew in every direction, some cast deliberately, some simply released in the whirlwind of combat.

Tortured screams, desperate cries and roars filled the chasm, which was living up to its name as a place of great and terrible suffering.

Then the tide began to turn.

In the end, the cavers were overwhelmed by the sheer numbers of the opposition. Peering out from beneath the crushed soldier, Gladius couldn't tell if the creatures had retreated or fallen in battle: one second the cavern was a tangled mess of furry backs and battered armour and the next it was just the glint of steel and lines of soldiers all standing in battle-ready positions.

Curse the gods, he thought. *That wiry old lunatic has won.*

He'd barely registered the observation when the dead soldier was heaved aside and he was dragged on to his feet.

Two rangy guards grimaced at him.

'Here's the fat one, Cap'n!'

Lich glared at Gladius across what remained of the battleground.

'Good. Now fetch the others and we'll take the lot o' 'em to Islaw.' He kicked the monkey skull into a dusty corner of the cavern. Then he limped over to Gladius and whispered into the

big slave's ear. 'Your smart idea just backfired
on you. Now those ignorant natives have fled,
it's time for you to suffer . . . and believe me, boy,
you and your friends *will* suffer.'

Decimus Rex was in a state of shock. He lay on
a crude wooden platform, fighting back tears of
anger and frustration as shadows danced from
the torches outside his temporary prison. The
last few hours had passed in a kind of tinted red
blur. He remembered fighting the cavers, and
being knocked unconscious during the
struggle, but everything else was hazy at best.
There were glimpses and images that filled in
the gaps in his memory: being passed from the
savage tribe to what appeared to be some sort of

private army, a troop of guards flanking him and dragging him into a fortress of some kind . . . and now, this, a dank, dark cell of the sort he guessed he should be getting used to after the trials in the arena.

However, it wasn't any of these fractured images that had so stunned the young gladiator. The only image causing Decimus such intense mental torment was the one visible from the tiny window in his cell.

He hadn't noticed it at first, until the cries from beyond the western wall had alerted him. He'd quickly climbed atop the bench and pulled himself up to the small barred window in order to see where the noises were coming from.

And there, suspended on the cavern wall by chains that wrapped around their arms and legs, were rows and rows of children. The entire wall looked like a scene from some twisted nightmare. Each line had to contain at least ten to fifteen chained slaves, and there were more than twice that number counting down, leading Decimus to the conclusion that he was looking upon *all* of the missing children. They must have been herded together like animals, he thought, before being quite literally *hung* on the walls of the cavern. Many of them were obviously starving, their ribs clearly visible through their flesh and their faces gaunt and hopeless. They had been abandoned here, presumably after failing whatever sickly, horrific purpose they had been snatched to fulfil.

Decimus found a boiling anger begin to rise within him, but he knew he would have to wait until they came for him. Only then would he get the chance to right this terrible wrong.

A sudden clamour shook him from his

thoughts. In the corridor outside the cell, the sound of approaching footfall grew steadily louder and louder.

Decimus leapt to his feet and felt every muscle in his body tightening. Releasing a deep breath, he steadied himself for some sort of attack from his captors, but instead of that, the cell door flew open and several prisoners were shoved, kicked and, in one case, *flung* inside.

Ruma, Argon, Teo and Olu landed heavily on the floor of the cell, still barely conscious as they tried and failed to get to their feet. Exhaustion quickly claimed all but one of them. Only Gladius was wide awake, but the slave had evidently suffered a brutal beating on his way to the cells. His face was a patchwork of purple bruises, and his right eye was badly swollen.

'I think,' he managed, wincing as a network of pain coursed through his jaw, 'we found the ones responsible for snatching those children.'

Decimus nodded at his oldest friend and, without breaking eye contact, raised one arm and pointed at the cell window. 'I reckon you might be right, there,' he said.

Two hours later, the rest of the slaves were beginning to come around. By the looks of things, Gladius had taken the worst beating. Teo and Argon were both tired and a little battered, but otherwise unhurt. Ruma and Olu hadn't been quite as lucky, and both had sustained deep cuts and bruises in their various fights with the demented cavers. None of them were complaining, however, when Decimus showed them the horrible view from the cell window.

'We have to get out of here,' Gladius managed. 'I overheard the soldiers talking. This fortress *does* belong to the Mirror Master, and he's been using it to carry out some sort of sick experiment on the children.'

Decimus nodded.

'That doesn't surprise me,' he growled. 'I'm guessing the kids chained to the wall outside are the ones who didn't make it.'

Gladius shook his head.

'NOBODY made it,' he said. 'He does something to the children, puts them in a fight with some sort of terrible enemy. They ALL fell in combat, so they're all worthless to him.'

'Do you think he'll try the same thing with

us?' Olu hazarded, massaging his arms.

'You can bet on it.' Gladius nodded, vehemently. 'I'm thinking that's probably why they took our blood.'

The others took a second to hear the big slave's words, but Decimus looked up immediately.

'What did you say? They took your *blood*?'

Gladius pointed at the underside of his arm. 'And yours, I'm guessing. The only reason I know they did it is because I was *awake*.'

Argon, Ruma, Olu and Teo all quickly discovered similar wounds on their own arms. Even Decimus had one.

'Why would they take our blood?' Argon asked.

Ruma's face became a mask of sudden disgust. 'You're right,' he said. 'We need to get out of here before we find out the answer to that question.'

Even as they spoke in the shadows of the cell, the slaves' blood was being transported to the highest tower in the fortress. Captain Lich, leading a group of heavy-set guards, marched into the chamber and commanded one of the men to bring forward the brass container he'd been carrying. The instruction was obeyed, and the container was placed on the room's single great bench.

A door on the opposite side of the tower creaked open, admitting the lean, rangy form of the Mirror Master.

He crossed the room in three long strides and came to stand before the gathering.

'You have all the samples, I trust?'

Captain Lich nodded. 'Yes, Islaw. All kept sep'rate, like you asked.'

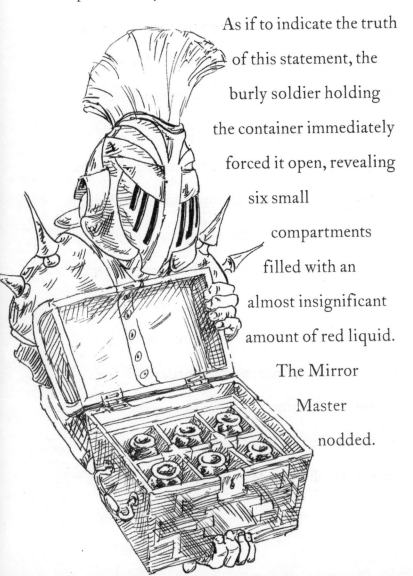

As if to indicate the truth of this statement, the burly soldier holding the container immediately forced it open, revealing six small compartments filled with an almost insignificant amount of red liquid. The Mirror Master nodded.

'Then we can proceed,' he said, turning to one of his own quiet servants. 'Bring out the Specials. Tell them . . . it's feeding time!'

The servant disappeared off into a narrow, sloping corridor that linked the east and west towers of the fortress. After a few minutes, he returned, leading a line of thin, unhealthy-looking youths. They all had sunken cheeks, watery eyes and teeth in various stages of decay. Their bones showed through their ragged clothing, and the flesh on their arms and legs was sallow, veins just visible beneath the surface.

The sight of them always made Lich feel slightly sick, but nothing compared to the revulsion he felt when they slowly began to transform. He shuddered as he looked upon them: only the gods knew what price Islaw had paid for the terrible, twisted ideas he had.

Slowly, one by one, the servants fed the Specials from the small, blood-filled containers. Then they were marched out of the tower and down to the Glass Arena.

CHAPTER
II

THE
GLASS
ARENA

Decimus had planned it out a dozen times: when the guards came for him, he would work out a plan of attack. When his friends were brought in, that plan just got bigger inside his head. As it turned out, however, when the guards *did* come for them, there were simply too many of them for any plan to work.

They literally poured into the small cell, taking the boys in teams and dragging them bodily along a maze of corridors towards a destination unknown to them.

Decimus tried to struggle, but the five men holding him had positioned themselves in such a tight net that any attempt to escape was immediately rendered futile. The others were suffering the same problem.

At length, the group rounded a final bend in the last passage and were brought before an immense set of double-doors. One of the guards detached himself from the rest of the unit and employed a large iron key to unlock the doors before flinging them wide. The boys were then snatched up once again and literally hurled inside.

It took them several seconds to dust themselves off and check for any injuries sustained during the transport. However, their minds were very quickly otherwise occupied by the incredible sights all around them.

Gladius gasped, Olu felt his jaw drop, Teo just stared, wide-eyed and even Ruma and Argon were speechless.

It was Decimus who finally spoke, but he

said, simply: 'What IS this place?'

The hall they now found themselves in was a fashioned arena of sorts, but the oddest arena any of the group had ever seen.

The upper section of the hall supported a circular seating area that ran around the length of the room, but the lower section was composed entirely of mirrors.

Decimus glanced around him, noting the glass panels in every direction, even covering the back of the doors they had entered through. The floor contained no panels, however – instead, it was one vast mirror section all by itself.

There looked to be hundreds of boys in the centre of the room, but in fact, every aspect of the walls and the floor merely reflected the six boys in their various positions and attitudes. The result was deeply unsettling, and very confusing.

'I don't know why we're in here,' Gladius whispered. 'But I think it might be best if we focus on the ceiling, or on each other: anything but the walls . . . and the floor.'

Decimus nodded, but he found the sight

almost impossible to ignore. Argon, Ruma, Teo and Olu were all having the same problem. The view was completely captivating.

It was only when a grim shout from the gallery above echoed all around the hall that the boys were shaken from their trances.

A slender man with long blond hair and strange, delicately proportioned armour was staring down at them. His features were oddly beautiful, and for a second, even keen-eyed Ruma thought he was looking upon the face of a girl.

However, the cold and harsh voice – when it sounded once again – soon corrected that impression.

'My name is Islaw Danis. I am a servant of the great Slavious Doom, and I am known in these parts as the Mirror Master. Looking around, my young friends, I am sure you can see why.'

Decimus said nothing, merely regarded the man with a disgusted expression. All around him, the others were doing the same.

Before the man spoke again, he was joined on the balcony by the awkward and darkly familiar form of Captain Lich, who spat on the floor several times as he tried and failed to cough some lodged filth from his lungs.

The Mirror Master ignored the arrival of his companion, and instead motioned toward the arena floor with a thin finger.

'Today, you are honoured to be the latest part of my most important experiment. As my master, the great Slavious Doom, would say—'

'LATE.'

Decimus bellowed the word so loudly that it echoed around the arena long after his lips had stopped moving.

The Mirror Master took a single breath, and glared at him.

'Would you care to repeat that?' he said, his voice even.

Decimus grinned.

'You said the "great" Slavious Doom, twice. I just wanted to correct you. He's actually the LATE Slavious Doom. I killed him just off Pin Yon Rock; he fell into the ocean and drowned.' He took several steps away from the rest of the group, just in case his words brought further danger upon them. 'I'm sorry to be the one to break it to you, but your master's reign of terror is OVER.'

Gladius felt himself beginning to shake as his friend's bold statement concluded. Argon, Teo, Olu and Ruma all exchanged worried glances.

However, the Mirror Master merely smiled and gently began to clap his hands together in some form of mock applause. Even Captain Lich's taught expression was edged with grim amusement.

'I love your spirit, young man,' said the Mirror Master, with a deep sigh. 'This contest will be absolutely fascinating.' He moved to sit down on the bench above the gallery, and then hesitated, as if remembering something important.

'Oh, and I'm sorry to be the one to break it to

you, but we have a very special guest joining us for today's experiment. I would introduce you, but I think you've met somewhere before?'

The gallery door behind him was suddenly wrenched open, admitting two burly guards. The men were both well over six foot tall, but were dwarfed by the towering figure they escorted on to the gallery.

The winged demon-helm was gone, as was the golden armour, but even in silver plate-mail, the form of Slavious Doom was immediately recognizable.

Argon almost fell over backwards. Ruma, Olu and Teo moved closer to each other for mutual support. Gladius shook his head as if dislodging something that had flown into his eye.

Decimus opened and closed his mouth several times before he found his voice.

'Y-you're dead!' he cried. 'I forced you over the side of the ship! I *watched* you sink beneath the waves.'

Doom's mouth split into a terrible grin.

'Young fool,' he spat. 'Brave enough to destroy me, and stupid enough not to stay in order to check that the job was done. You left the remains of my men at Pin Yon Rock. They rescued me, and D'Tong's fastest ship saw me safely back where I belong. RIGHT HERE.'

Doom let out a deafening roar of a laugh which echoed all around the arena.

'Today, Decimus Rex,' he said, his voice filled with demonic mirth, 'I will watch the creations of my greatest apprentice reduce you and your friends to mere snivelling wrecks . . . and then I will pay a long overdue visit to your parents. You have caused me suffering and humiliation, boy, and in doing so you have forced me to make an example of *them*. They will be cast into the fires of Mount Vesuvius as a warning to other slaves, like yourself, who think to stand against me.'

A deadly silence settled on the arena floor. Everyone wanted to speak up for Decimus, who was now literally shaking with rage.

'You will not lay a *hand* on my parents,' Decimus thundered. 'If you do, I swear to the gods you will pay with your life.'

Doom smiled. 'So speaks the Chosen One! The one destined to retrieve the Blade of Fire! Oh, yes, but you failed – didn't you?

Hahahahahahaha!'

The overlord slapped his apprentice on the shoulder, and the Mirror Master quickly gestured to his servants. As the gathered minions of Slavious Doom took their seats, a slow, grinding noise filled the arena. It sounded as though a vast machine was working somewhere just out of sight.

Gladius immediately spotted the movement of the mirrors. Each great wall panel had become a revolving column, with identical mirrors on every side ... so now, not only were the reflections multiplied, they were *moving*, too.

Argon leapt into a fighting stance, as if he half expected a rain of boiling rocks to be hurled on him from some unseen quarter. Olu,

Ruma and Teo all followed his example, quickly readying themselves for combat.

Only Decimus remained absolutely still, glaring up at the distant form of Slavious Doom with all-consuming hatred.

My parents, he thought. *I should never have left my parents. How could I have been so stupid ... so arrogant?*

'Decimus!' Gladius yelled, realizing his friend hadn't even *seen* the walls start to rotate. 'Snap out of it! We need you here!'

When he got no reply from his friend, he marched up to him and slapped him hard on the back.

Decimus jumped, and instinctively raised his fists.

'I'm sorry,' Gladius muttered. 'But we've got problems – look!'

The walls were now moving at a slow but steady pace, spinning the many reflections into one incredible carousel of images.

It was at that very moment that the Specials

arrived in the hall. They stepped out from behind the spinning columns, creeping towards the group with careful, deliberate steps ... and they might as well have been completely invisible, for none of the boys could see them.

'What is that long-haired idiot waiting for?' Olu shouted, peering around him in every direction.

'I don't like this,' Ruma growled. 'Something's wrong.'

Argon nodded. 'Why is nothing happening? I'd have expected wild animals or at least a rack of spikes by now.'

Decimus and Gladius were both circling each other, trying not to get too disorientated by the world of reflections spinning all around them.

Teo was a good head shorter than all his

friends, and had been focusing largely on his own reflection. Unobserved by the rest of the group, he stalked the nearest mirrored column, moving very slowly and watching his reflection move likewise. It was only when he was practically on top of the column that he noticed something very odd: his reflection was bleeding. A tiny trickle of blood ran from between Teo's lips and, on impulse, he raised a finger to wipe it away.

When he glanced down, however, there was no blood on his finger. Not even the tiniest spec.

He looked up again, and the reflection drove a fist straight into his face.

Teo flew into the air and crashed on to the glass floor, spinning around several times as the reflection leapt after him.

'What on earth?' Gladius grabbed Decimus and spun him around to face the unfolding situation, a situation that was difficult to see and practically impossible to believe.

The two Teos looked exactly the same, only they didn't: not really . . . not at all. The *reflections* of the two boys were identical, but the reality – difficult though it was to separate from the countless images all around them – was very different. The boy moved like Teo and was even, strangely, *shaped* like Teo . . . but he wasn't Teo.

As the observation hit home, Decimus immediately dashed over to help his friend, but was suddenly attacked by his own reflection and sent flying by a kick that slammed directly into the centre of his chest. He hadn't even seen the boy approach.

All around the hall, similar attacks were taking place. In one corner of the room, Olu found himself inside his *own* headlock. Argon and Ruma were trying and failing to avoid chops and strikes from *themselves*. Even Gladius found his path blocked by an equally large imitation, a kind of hollow-faced double

that drove a back-handed slap across his face with such force that his eyes streamed with water.

Up in the gallery, Doom was cackling with

evil laughter, while Lich smirked and the Mirror Master looked incredibly satisfied with his efforts.

Decimus tried to focus on his attack, ignoring the many reflections that made it feel as though was fighting twenty identical foes.

On top of everything else, the boy he was fighting was decidedly ... weird. He seemed to know what Decimus would do before he actually did it. Every punch was blocked, every kick swept aside, every chop countered with a strike that

invariably left him injured and gasping for air. It wasn't that the boy was a brilliant fighter, more that he had the same *instincts* as Decimus. It was like playing a mind game . . . against yourself.

Decimus went for a desperate lunge, using all his strength to drive a double-handed chop at his opponent . . . but the boy anticipated his move perfectly, stepping aside at the last second and employing Decimus's own weight to flip him on to his back.

The young gladiator hit the glass floor with a thud, causing a network of hairline cracks to appear in the glass.

All over the arena, the group was being defeated.

Ruma tried everything to escape the headlock he found himself in, quickly resorting to a lift

which sent both himself and the other boy

crashing on to the glass floor. However, at the

last second he found the move reversed and the

boy actually landed on top of him, his elbow

firmly in Ruma's neck. The pain was excruciating, and made all the more difficult to take because Ruma remembered using the same move on several of his own opponents in the past.

Argon was being matched in both speed and strength. Always relying on his muscular arms to force any enemy to their knees, he resorted to a Roman knuckle lock, only to find himself rapidly losing. Legs bent slightly as he was forced down, Argon tried to dodge as the boy ducked under him and back-flipped him on to the floor. There was a crash, and the widening cracks in the glass doubled.

Olu and Teo, the fastest members of the group, were being outpaced.

Teo dodged every strike with his

customary agility, but seemed to find a rain of blows waiting for him *wherever* he landed. Realizing that he needed to treble his efforts, he went for a running kick that had never failed him in the past. Shockingly, however, the boy he was fighting met him in mid-air with the *same* move. They both slammed on to the floor, but Teo had taken the worst of the blow and found the wind completely knocked out of him. His opponent, by contrast, was back on his feet in seconds.

Olu's favourite method of attack was a leg sweep he'd perfected while training himself for the horrors of the arena. He performed the set-up for the move perfectly, driving a fist into the stomach of his opponent and following it up with a kick to the back of the ankles. Then, as his opponent flipped back on to his feet, he dropped to the floor and swept his legs around at an impossible speed.

The boy jumped. He actually *jumped* before Olu's feet reached the back of his legs. Moreover, he landed with a well-aimed fist in Olu's side. The gangly slave screamed in agony. It was exactly the move he would have done in the circumstances.

A short distance away, Gladius hit a wall mirror with such force that it shattered. He'd decided to use all his weight in a running attack on his opponent, but the clash had actually thrown *him* backwards. Glass exploded all around him, as one by one the mirrors all around the walls came crashing down like dominos. It cleared the view in every direction, but the sudden lack of confusion meant nothing.

Gladius was cut to ribbons, Olu writhed in agony, Teo was barely conscious, Ruma gasped for breath like a fish out of water, Argon was curled up, moaning loudly, and Decimus was trying and failing to get to his feet.

All around them, the Specials took up battle stances, but they had no one to fight.

The slaves had been soundly defeated. They were simply no match for the Mirror Master's strange and deadly warriors.

'Bravo!' Doom yelled, patting his grinning apprentice on the back and then clapping his hands together in a round of generous applause. 'At last we find the fighters who can beat these infuriating thorns in my side.'

The overlord rose to his feet.

'And now, my friends, I am afraid I have pressing business elsewhere. After all, young Decimus's parents will not throw themselves into the flames, now will they?' He turned to his apprentice and the smirking Captain Lich. 'Come with me. It's time we left this fetid hole you call a fortress.'

The Mirror Master glanced from the arena to Doom, and back again.

'What of the slaves, my lord?' he enquired. 'We have two hundred on the walls, outside, and these . . . unfortunates in here.'

Doom smiled down at Decimus and his defeated friends.

'Captain Lich and his guards can have the

pleasure of executing the ones on the walls,' he growled. 'And you can have your Specials finish these *insects*: their deaths are long overdue.'

As Doom and Lich headed out of the gallery, the Mirror Master gave one last command to his victorious creations.

'Finish them,' he said.

CHAPTER III

THE TIDE TURNS

Hope had faded for the group. After so many victories, they now found themselves weary, sapped of energy by the sheer unthinking skill of their opponents.

Only Decimus had the will to carry on, struggling to his feet and expelling one last burst of energy in a rain of punches and kicks. Every single blow was countered and he was struck so hard by a wild, back-handed swing that his vision actually shimmered as he collapsed on to the glass.

The Specials moved silently around the group, each stalking their own prey. They were taking their time, watching for any attempts at sudden movement.

'It's no good,' Ruma shouted. 'They can

anticipate everything we do. It's over! We're finished!'

Gladius rolled on to his stomach, wiped some blood from his eyes and was about to prepare himself for the final assault when the boy before him came into sharp focus for the first time. He looked a little like Gladius, and moved *exactly* like Gladius . . . and, on reflection, it was practically impossible to outmanoeuvre *yourself*.

'Swap!' Gladius screamed, leaping to his feet and moving *away* from his own attacker. 'Everyone fight a *different* opponent.'

The group took a second to register Gladius's urgent message, but then – finally – the penny seemed to drop. They quickly scrambled to their feet.

Ruma leapfrogged prone companions and slammed into Decimus's Special. Teo took on Gladius's stalking opponent, while Olu flew into Argon's reflective enemy. The Gaul took on Ruma's leftover clone, while Decimus ploughed into Olu's likeness, leaving Gladius with the small and deadly character who'd been out-dodging Teo.

Suddenly, the one-sided combat in the hall exploded into a full-blown war.

Decimus knew all of Olu's weaknesses in combat. He'd watched his friend fight on countless occasions, and could ably predict most of the gangly slave's various methods of attack. The first punch was easily predictable: Decimus snatched hold of the Special's wrist and twisted it in several manic turns. Then he drove a knee into the boy's side and finished him off with an open-handed blow to the chin that had so much power behind it that it actually took the Special off his feet and turned him in a complete somersault.

The Olu imitation lost consciousness when he hit the glass, and Decimus saw a remarkable change come over the boy. Everything that was in any way *Olu*-like about the Special seemed to melt away, leaving a sick and pallid-looking youth lying on the floor, a few specks of blood around his lips.

Gladius had always wondered how he would ever deal with someone of Teo's speed and agility. The trick, he decided, was just to wait ... not to throw any effort into trying to keep up with the little Special. It soon paid off. Gladius threw a number of effortless punches which all flew wide of the mark. All the while, he watched how the boy jumped and darted around: left, right, up, down, leap, dodge, duck ... SLAM.

Gladius let rip with the most powerful punch he'd ever thrown, purely guessing where Teo's clone *would* be in the next blink of his eye. He was right. The big slave's meaty fist cannoned into the boy's face, knocking him out, cold.

The deflated, defeated clone hit the ground with a dull thud, sliding into a fractured part of the mirrored floor even as his skin sagged and the weight seemed to shrink from his arms and legs.

Argon snatched Ruma's Special off the ground and hurled him into the only remaining mirror column, sending out a shower of glass that flew in every direction. As the clone recovered from the collision and struggled to his feet, Gladius joined Argon and together they easily overpowered him.

Teo was easily outmanoeuvring Gladius's Special, but landing a solid blow on the boy was proving decidedly difficult, as his flesh seemed to absorb every determined strike the little slave made. In the end, he ducked two clumsy punches and leapt on to the larger boy's back, trying to apply a headlock while at the same time putting himself in a position where he could not easily be grappled. As he jumped and interlocked his arms around the clone's head, Decimus himself roared into the combat, slamming a series of single-handed blows into the boy's stomach. Working as a team, they forced the Gladius Special on to his knees and knocked the wind, and the consciousness, out of him.

As the group began to seriously overwhelm their formerly indestructible opponents, Ruma and the Decimus clone were fighting up a storm in the middle of the room.

Ruma was used to fighting Decimus. He'd
chosen to take on his old friend's clone because
he *knew* he was the only member of the group
who had any chance of beating the young
gladiator in combat.

Using every trick he'd learned in his real-life clashes with Decimus, he ducked and weaved with careful precision, allowing the clone's instinctive reflections of the young gladiator's confident attacks to trick him into making a mistake. Just like Decimus, the clone surged forward every time, roaring like a lion and throwing fast and furious punches. Unfortunately, he also possessed Decimus's single weakness: over-confidence. Ruma faked a dramatic reaction to a punch that hadn't actually done him that much damage. He pretended to stagger, half-dazed, and when the clone flew in to finish him off, he spun around and delivered an awe-inspiring high kick directly to the boy's jaw.

The Decimus clone genuinely staggered, and

Ruma finished him off with a plain and simple punch that he was certain would never have taken the *real* Decimus Rex off his feet.

The slaves staggered around for a few seconds, stumbling in the hall like a group of wounded, bewildered travellers moving through swampy ground.

'Th-thank the gods for you, my friend,' Decimus said, nodding at the big slave. 'Never stop thinking for us, will you?'

Gladius managed a weak grin, and shrugged. 'What do we do now?'

A dark look drifted into the eyes of Decimus Rex. 'I need to stop Doom killing my parents, and finish him once and for all . . . but there's something else I need to do first.'

'Then what are we waiting for?' said Ruma,

determinedly. The scrawny Etrurian made to move off, but Decimus grabbed his arm and held him back.

'It's really important that you all do as I say,' he pressed, preparing himself for the inevitable argument. 'I need to leave right now, and I need to take Argon with me.'

'But—'

'Me?' The Gaul looked momentarily surprised. 'Why? What can I—'

'You're the strongest,' Decimus continued. 'And I'm going to need strength where I'm going. The rest of you ...' he turned to face Gladius, Teo, Olu and Ruma, 'must free those children.'

Teo and Ruma shared a worried glance, but it was Olu – usually the most passive of the group

– who almost exploded with anger.

'Four of us against Lich and his army? That's insane, Decimus! It's suicide – even together we'd end up with a nightmare on our hands! Without you and Argon, what chance do we stand? All those children will die.'

Decimus swallowed a few times, but it was Gladius who spoke.

'Don't worry, Olu,' he said. 'We will get the children out – I know just how to do it.' The big slave turned to Decimus and patted his oldest friend on the back. 'You and Argon do what you need to save your parents, and we will come and find you when we've rescued the slaves on the wall.'

The group parted ways, Olu still muttering about *impossible tasks* and even Ruma and Teo looking unusually despondent. Only Gladius had a sly smile on his face, and it seemed he wasn't about to let the others in on his secret. He snatched a torch from a wall sconce outside the fortress, and made for the depths of the chasm.

CHAPTER
IV

THE
WALL

C aptain Lich was employing his bizarre half-limping gait in order to stay ahead of the troop of soldiers he was leading. His wooden splint clicked on the cavern floor behind the fortress as the incredible sight of the prisoners came into view.

The cries of pain from the multitude of children chained to the rocks fell on deaf ears, as Lich ordered the soldiers to divide into two groups and sent them off in different directions, supplying each leader with a heavy set of iron keys.

'Use the footholds to climb each row to the top!' he shouted. 'Unlock one end of the chains and the whole line will collapse: they can all fall to their deaths. It's the quickest way.'

A bodyguard leaned over to mumble into his

superior's ragged ear. 'What about the ones on the lower rows, Cap'n?'

Lich shrugged. 'Just get rid o' 'em,' he said. 'I don' care 'ow it's done.'

The two sets of guards reached the footholds on each respective side of the cavern and began to climb their way up to the higher chain lines. Lich watched them with a mixture of excitement and annoyance. He'd always hated children, but he'd far rather have seen the boy's parents thrown into the volcano with the master himself. *This* was a job for the common grunts, not for a captain.

The two leading soldiers had reached the highest line of slaves. Ignoring the terrified, pleading cries of the children, the man on the right side of the line unhooked his keys and reached across to unlock the first chain. He put the key into the lock, took a deep breath and then prepared to undo the chains.

He didn't make it.

There was a sudden flashing blur, a deathly scream and the man was blasted from his footholds and sent plummeting to his death on the rock floor below. The keys rattled in the lock, but didn't fall after him.

Lich started in shock as, all over the cavern, the cavers appeared, swinging down on lengths of vine and springing from openings high up in the rock face. They were all screaming war cries and moving so fast that they looked like one giant mass of hair and muscle.

As they dropped from their perches and ploughed into the rest of the soldiers, Lich

staggered back and glanced around him for the
source of this new chaos.

There, at the back of the cavern, standing just
inside the shadows of the fortress, were four
members of the slave group from the Mirror
Hall . . . and the fat one was carrying the

re-ignited monkey skull!

As he looked on, Teo and Ruma rushed forward, snaking around the dread captain and hurtling towards the wall.

'Kill 'em!' Lich screamed at the top of his voice, twisting around on his splint. 'Kill 'em all!' He limped closer to the base of the wall and screamed up at the soldiers still on the rock-face. 'Unlock that line! I want those wailing wretches dead!'

The guard now at the top of the line hastened up the last few footholds and took hold of the key, but he slipped and his fingers fumbled with the lock.

Teo darted up the wall like a spider monkey, taking the footholds two at a time. In the blink of an eye, he had scrambled over the backs of several soldiers and was now grappling with the leading guard, trying to headlock the man before he got a renewed grip on the keys.

Unfortunately, he couldn't quite wrestle the soldier's muscular arm down from the chain, and there was a sickening click as the key turned.

Thinking on his feet, Teo snatched at the unravelling line and quickly wrapped a length of it around the guard. The weight of the tumbling line dragged the man off the wall, taking Teo – still clinging fast – with him.

The chain collapsed, and twenty screaming children slid directly downwards in a catastrophic drop. However, Teo's quick thinking had saved their lives: the soldier at the end of the line hung mere feet from the ground, his limp body forming a stopper that brought all the children to a halt. They formed a squashed line behind the man, as Teo moved off his shoulders and attempted to unwrap the chain.

All over the cavern, soldiers were clashing with the enraged and vengeful cavers ... but this time the battle was very different. Spurred on by their flaming idol, the cavers were fighting with renewed determination and several flourishes that took the assembled soldiers completely by surprise.

Swords were drawn and lost as the swinging cavers flew over the heads of the soldiery, snatching the men from the ground and hurling them high into the air. Other members of the tribal clan simply dropped from the vines and crashed into random groups of soldiers, using their powerful limbs to pummel, crush and defeat their enemies.

Realizing that the battle was going against him, Lich drew his own sword and headed for the rocky crest where Gladius was still holding aloft the flaming monkey skull and screaming commands. He covered the distance between them in practically no time at all, and was just reaching up to dislodge the big slave from his lofty position when Olu cannoned into him. Lich flew backwards, his sword cast aside, and landed heavily with the gangly slave still on top of him.

Up on the far side of the wall, Ruma had wrestled the second set of keys from the other guard leader and was picking his way along the slave-line, assisted in places by the chained children who all cheered him on as he passed.

The cavers were winning the battle: their ambush had taken the guards completely by surprise. To add to their frustrations, Teo and the twenty slaves he'd freed from the top line had snatched up the swords of fallen soldiers and were weighing into the fray, the boys screaming with weeks of pent-up hatred and rage.

Gladius stood his ground on the rock, holding the fiery skull aloft with a nervous but determined look on his face: he knew he had to maintain firm command of the tribe, but was equally worried that Olu wouldn't be able to handle the dreaded Captain Lich alone.

As it turned out, he couldn't have been more right. Lich flipped Olu effortlessly over his head and, employing his sword as a support, forced himself back on to his feet. When the lanky slave leapt up again, Lich caught him a vicious swipe across the lower jaw. Olu staggered sideways, but Lich was only getting *started*. The captain put all the weight on his good leg, and drove the splint into the boy's midsection, finishing Olu off with an elbow to the jaw which sent the slave flying into a pile of jagged rocks. Never one to give a wounded opponent time to catch his breath, Lich crossed the path in a remarkably quick shamble, snatched hold of Olu's neck and yanked him back on to his feet, slamming a head-butt into the side of the gangly slave's face and knocking him off his feet once again.

Gladius watched the fight with mounting horror, increasingly aware that the cavers had nearly finished their assault on the army.

'Ruma!' he screamed, suddenly observing that the scrawny Etrurian had successfully retrieved the keys and was now climbing down to the bottom of the cavern wall. 'Help Olu! Quick!'

Ruma landed on his feet and peered around wildly, searching for his friend. When his eyes fixed on Lich, who was reaching down to snatch Olu up for a third time, he bolted across the path like a possessed animal, slamming into the captain with enough force to drive the hollow wretch off his feet. Lich scrabbled around in the dirt, but the wily Etrurian was characteristically relentless, and immediately drove two kicks pointedly into the older man's stomach. Lich rolled over and over on the dusty ground, then spotted the sword he had dropped during Olu's first attack. He gritted his teeth and made a frantic crawl to retrieve it. Ruma leapt over his head and landed on the blade, swiftly stamping on Lich's fingers when the captain tried to grab the pommel.

'Argh! You demonic little—'

The captain's words were cut short by his own sudden movement, a spinning, one-legged sweep which took Ruma by surprise and knocked him off his feet. Lich cackled with the

sheer glee of combat and smashed a fist into the boy's knee, causing Ruma to cry out as he scrambled away, trying to avoid any further attacks.

Lich rolled over and clawed along the ground after him, but suddenly stopped, his eyes bulging in his head.

'Arghgghghghghghghghghghghghghgh!'

He gasped, spat out a few strangled words that made no sense whatsoever and, finally, slumped forward, the life gone out of him.

Ruma, still moving along on his belly, peered behind him to see what had stopped the captain's eager pursuit.

Lich was lying face down in the dirt, his own sword driven hard into his back. Olu was still clutching the blade-handle, his lips twisted in a terrible grimace.

'You evil, black-hearted fiend,' he growled. 'Murder children, would you? Not now, you won't.' He relaxed his weight on the weapon and staggered back, offering a hand to Ruma who gladly took his friend's help.

The battle in the cavern was over. Still bellowing cries of well-earned victory, the cavers took care of the last few soldiers and then, following Gladius's equally booming commands, helped Teo to get the remaining slaves to safety. They crawled up and down the walls, seemingly clinging to the weakest and most insignificant of handholds, in order to put two, sometimes three children on to their backs in one attempt. Ruma and Teo unlocked every chain, manacle and leg-iron fixed to the mass of gathered children, while Gladius marched directly up to the enormous leader of the caver tribe.

'Here,' he said, thrusting the flaming monkey skull towards the behemoth. 'I believe this rightfully belongs to you.'

There was a moment of grim hesitation, before the caver understood ... and eagerly took possession of the sacred relic.

Gladius bowed before him. 'We owe you thanks. May your gods protect you always.'

Then, as the tribe withdrew from the chasm, disappearing into various caves up and down the rocky walls of the cavern, Gladius turned to the newly-freed slaves with a tired but very relieved smile on his face. Ruma and Teo came to stand beside him, but Olu strode past the assembled group and climbed up on to the rock that Gladius had stood on to command the cavers.

'You are all free,' the gangly slave shouted, his voice echoing all around the rocks. 'And you will be as eager to return to your homes as we are!'

There was a roar of approval from the crowd, but when Olu raised a hand, his concerned expression soon provoked a hush of quiet. 'However, the leader of the group who came to rescue you is a boy called Decimus Rex, a great hero who is, even now, on his way to save his parents from your captor and his master, the evil Slavious Doom. I ask nothing more of you than to go free and live your lives, but for those of you who wish to stay with us and fight . . . I would welcome your help to make every child in our great land FREE!'

For a moment, there was nothing but silence. Teo and Ruma swallowed, and even Gladius looked down at his feet.

Olu took two of the longest breaths he'd ever taken, searching the gathered army of slaves for anything that might pass as a sign that his words had been understood.

Then, a very small boy at the front of the crowd stepped forward and cried, simply:

'FREE!'

'FREE!' came another shout, and then the voices doubled.

Trebled.

Multiplied beyond measure.

Every voice in the cavern was unified.

'FREE!'

'FREE!'

'FREEEEEEEEEEEEEEEEEEEE!'

Far above the chasm of the Screaming Void and several miles from the forest that concealed it, Decimus and Argon managed to keep time with each other's fast pace. They crossed hills and valleys, past towns and settlements, and still they ran on.

'So we're not going to your parents' village?' the Gaul asked, his arms pumping the air as he sped along.

'There's no point,' Decimus breathed. 'Doom has a lead on us; he will take them prisoner and have them transported to Mount Vesuvius for their execution. It will take him time, of course ... enough time for us to find something first.'

'And what's that, exactly?'

Decimus grinned as he ran. 'We're going to find the Blade of Fire,' he said.

GLADIATOR GAME

THE WALL RACE

In this very quick but exciting game, one player
takes on the role of Teo, while the other plays a
Roman guard in charge of unlocking the
prisoners and letting them fall to their deaths!
Can you repeat the heroic actions of the little
slave and save the children as he did, or will
they be doomed in this game? To play, you will
need two dice, a pencil and a piece of paper.
Note: this game is difficult to win, as the evil
soldier has the advantage!

First, Teo must catch the soldier, who is

already a good distance ahead of him. The cliff-face has fifty footholds. You will need to make a note of the scores as they increase! First, roll two dice for the soldier, giving you a score between 2 and 12. The score is how many footholds the soldier has climbed. Then, roll ONE die for Teo, adding 3 to the score because he is so fast!

If Teo reaches the top first (i.e. gets to 50 or above before the soldier), he has successfully grabbed the keys and must now try to escape immediately. However, there is a two in six chance of Teo falling as he attempts to leap on to the chain-line. You must shout out two numbers and then roll the die. If you get any number *other* than the two you shouted, Teo has survived and has rescued the prisoners. If you get one of the numbers you shouted, Teo has fallen to his doom.

If the soldier reaches the keys first, he must quickly unlock the chains. However, there is a slim chance he will fumble and drop the keys! You must shout out one number and then roll the die. If you get any number *other* than the one you shouted, the soldier has been successful and all the children have fallen to their doom. If you get the exact number you shouted, the keys have fallen and you have lost.

CHARACTER PROFILE
THE MIRROR MASTER

NAME: Islaw Danis, the Mirror Master

FROM: Parts unknown

HEIGHT: 1.56 metres

BODY TYPE: Lean, rangy

Fact File: The Mirror Master was Slavious Doom's first and most trusted apprentice.
The Mirror Master always wanted to be a great conjurer as a child, but could never discover true magic.
The Mirror Master loves puzzles and games, especially if they are deadly and involve pain.

MIRROR MASTER QUIZ: How well do you know Islaw Danis? Can you answer the following questions?

1. WHO IS THE ONLY PERSON TO CALL THE MIRROR MASTER BY HIS REAL NAME?
2. WHO IS THE MIRROR MASTER'S SURPRISE GUEST DURING THE BATTLE IN THE GLASS ARENA?
3. WHAT DOES THE MIRROR MASTER FEED HIS SPECIALS?

Answers: 1. Captain Lich **2.** Slavious Doom **3.** The blood of future opponents.

COMING SOON
GLADIATOR BOY

A terrible race has begun, one that will lead to either victory or tragedy for young gladiator, Decimus Rex. Either Decimus will recover the lost Blade of Fire and save his parents from the evil Slavious Doom, or else his worst fears will be realized.

As Olu and Gladius lead an army of child slaves in pursuit of Doom's men and their leader, the twisted Mirror Master, they wonder if they will be in time to stop the slaughter and if this is truly a battle they can win...

To find out more, read on in the first chapter of...

GLADIATOR BOY vs THE ULTIMATE EVIL

CHAPTER
I

THE
RETURN
TO
PRIMUS

'It's so much worse than I thought.'

Decimus peered over the ridge and looked down at the valley that had once contained the dreaded Arena of Doom. Now, all that remained of the great and terrible building was a massive pile of rubble that stretched as far as the eye could see in every direction. From the way rocks were strewn around the edge of the valley, it looked as if the arena had mostly collapsed outwards, though Decimus could definitely remember wandering through the tunnels beneath, feeling as though the place was caving *in* above him.

'Look,' Argon whispered, pointing down at a wide and tall section of rubble that had presumably been the very centre of Arena Primus. 'Doom's men are *still* here.'

Sure enough, it was true. An entire legion of the overlord's soldiers was wading through the debris in one part of the ruin, while teams of guards in another shifted heavy blocks of stone into piles.

'Do you think they're rebuilding the place?' the Gaul continued. 'It certainly looks like there's some sort of mission to—'

'They're looking for the Blade of Fire,' said Decimus, a grim assurance in his voice. 'Doom still desperately wants it, and wouldn't forget about it just to get his revenge upon *me*.'

The young gladiator turned to his friend with a sly smile. 'They won't find it, though. When the Maw swallowed it and sank into the depths of the earth, a thousand tons of rubble collapsed on top of the thing. It's going to take them years even to get through the *top* layer.'

Argon frowned.

'Then how are we supposed to find it?' he ventured.

'Because we know something they don't. We walked no more than six or seven tunnels in order to get out before the arena collapsed.

Sure, they were steep and really difficult to get through . . . but we still survived, and when we emerged into daylight, we weren't anywhere near where they're digging.' Decimus turned slightly and pointed toward the far end of the valley, at a barely visible pile of outlying rubble. 'We were over there.'

Argon allowed his gaze to follow his friend's pointed finger, and beamed an equally sly smile. 'So we were!'

'Let's go.'

The two companions hurried around the top of the ridge and swiftly navigated the higher foothills that sloped down to the valley floor, picking their way carefully through clearings that might have been visible to the soldiers far below.

Staying out of sight in the lower hills, Decimus and Argon found their way to the outlying rubble in no time at all, and immediately began to shift some of the smaller rocks blocking a patch of ground that Decimus was sure covered the exit they'd come through on that fateful day, two years before.

An hour passed in the sweltering sunlight, but the heavy, exhausting labour bore no fruit ... and still there were more rocks.

After a second hour, however, Argon suddenly hefted aside a massive rock and stopped dead.

'Here!' he said, almost jumping up and down with glee. 'There's a hole right here!'

Decimus joined his friend. Sure enough, there was an opening visible beneath the stones,

just large enough to accommodate one of them
at a time.

'What are we waiting for?' Argon said,
wriggling down into the hole before Decimus
could even muster a reply.

The young gladiator took one last glance
toward the distant soldiers, and followed.

The tunnel was hot and impossibly dark,

with only a sliver of light from the hole to illuminate their passage.

'We're going to need a torch,' Argon muttered as he almost tripped over a stack of rocks that were blocking the path.

Decimus shook his head. 'No, we can't afford to waste any more time messing about,' he said. 'The Maw's cavern had a natural green light that swelled up from the beast itself. As soon as we get close we should be able to see . . . if it's still alive.'

Argon gasped in the darkness. 'You're not serious?' he muttered. 'How do you expect to find your way back to the cavern in the pitch dark? It's *impossible.*'

Decimus moved past the Gaul and patted his friend companionably on the shoulder.

'Nothing's impossible,' he said. 'Besides, I remember these tunnels from the escape. I don't know why; maybe, deep down, I had a feeling I'd be back here, someday. Hell, maybe the prophecy *is* right.'

GLADIATOR BOY

WWW.GLADIATORBOY.COM

Have you checked out the Gladiator Boy website? It's the place to go for games, downloads, activities, sneak previews and lots of fun!

Sign up to the newsletter at **WWW.GLADIATORBOY.COM** and receive exclusive extra content and the opportunity to enter special members-only competitions.